SHORT TAKES

SHORT TAKES

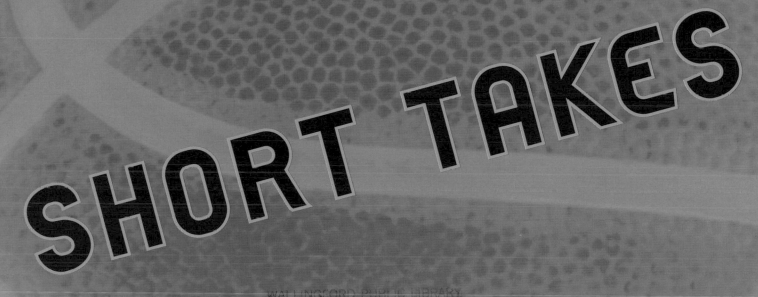

Charles R. Smith Jr.

Dutton Children's Books 🏀 New York

FAST~BREAK
BASKETBALL
POETRY

TO THE MEMORY OF MY FATHER,
Charles Robert Smith Sr.,
WHO TAUGHT ME TO ALWAYS KEEP MY EYES ON THE GOAL

ACKNOWLEDGMENTS

This book would not have been possible without the help of so many people who gave me their time, energy, and effort to accomplish what you see here.

A big thanks goes to Maria and Ivana Palma for rounding up the troops for another book: Christina Ricchetti, Lisa Puccio, and Lisa and Nicole Iannotto. Thanks for enduring the heat and my camera.

I also need to thank several of the players on the Central Park courts in New York City who let me capture their moves, even though that sometimes meant missing a game. Thanks to my Brooklyn neighbor Mike, who represented Croatia to the fullest.

And a special thanks goes to my wife, Gillian, who was my second pair of eyes and hands when I needed to have my picture taken and who acted as my model for some pictures that she didn't understand.

Thanks to all of you for chopping this monumental task down to bite-sized pieces and for all the fun I had with you in the process.

CIP Data is available.
Published in the United States 2001 by Dutton Children's Books,
a division of Penguin Putnam Books for Young Readers
345 Hudson Street, New York, New York 10014
www.penguinputnam.com
Designed by Ellen M. Lucaire
Printed in Hong Kong
First Edition
1 2 3 4 5 6 7 8 9 10
ISBN 0-525-46454-9

Contents

They call me

the show
stopper

the dime
dropper

the
spin move to the left
reverse jam **popper**

The high
flier

on the high
wire.

6

HELLO
my name is

The intense
rim-rattlin'
noise
amplifier.

The net-**shaker**
back
board **breaker**
creator
of the funky dunk
hip-**shaker.**

The Man
Sir Slam
The Legend
I be.

That's just
a few of the
names
they call **me.**

Rainmaker steps
on court
to perform
stirring thunder
gray clouds
ready to storm.

Strong gusts of wind
the storm does begin
the stronger the better to create great spin.

Lightning strikes first
and thunder roars past
a downpour of jump shots is in the forecast.

8

Clouds burst forth and drop balls of rain

that fall from above and splash through the chains.

Buckets of points are piling up quick

the court is now soaked and the asphalt is slick.

The Rainmaker's shower has left others wet
and all this was done
without breaking a sweat.

The trick to the ball

spinning your name on the net:

a flick of the wrist.

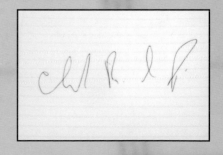

Brooklyn

In the county of Kings
defense rules
and the

"baby I'm a star"
school
is out.

No doubt
when a
high-flying jam

is stopped

offense is cool

a mark
is left
that proves

and
thrown out
of the park

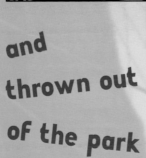

blocked

but defense

still rules.

Sneakers squeak

on Floors

made of teak,

but as squeaks

14

a sound

all its own. ◉

Shadow Dancing

16

in the
trance

Shadows
dance
and prance

of my opponent
in the
defensive
stance.

Legs **move**
arms **groove**

stop
pop
and **drop**
2
on **you**

to rhythm
that puts my
body
in the
mood to

while
your shadow
dances
to the

beat
of
my **groove.**

"**D**idn't I see a picture of your

jump shot on

the back of a milk carton?"

"Your game is like ice cream

on a hot summer day—soft!"

"I must be buttah
'cause I'm on a roll!"

"I'm **lightin'** you up like a **pinball machine!**"

"Were you guardin' me?"

"That's **off!**"
"Yeah, **off** the **backboard** into the net!"

"**They call me Cream** 'cause I always rise to the top."

"You better get your **umbrella** 'cause I'm raining all over you!"

S hake
left.

I shake
to the
left.

To the
left

I shake

and break

ankles
like
sticks.

My tricks
too smooth

I school
fools

on the
finer
points of
my
"J."

From way
outside
I
bust a
trey

look at
you

smile

and say

"All
day!"

Slippery slidin'
soles
make molds

of tires
burnin' tracks.
CRACRACK
ankles snap

back
as
the bull charges
to the rack.

Strong and sturdy
limbs spin
and

22

cock the
hammer and
crush
the tin. 🏀

elevate
and levitate
toward the rim

like a cape.
I don't
hesitate I
motivate

spin again
the wind
around me

Perched in hiding like a hawk
eyes on prey, ready to stalk.

Predator poised,
ready to go
nose drops down,
ready to swing low.

Arms once stretched
now cling tight
legs like jets
coil for flight.

Hawk swoops down, feathery wings fall
silent and swift and pounce on the ball.

Quick like the wind, predator takes prey
and retreats to the nest until the next play.

The soft leather pings
the hard asphalt like a drum;

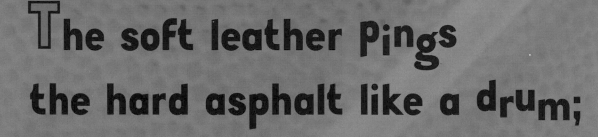

fast

and in control.

Like the sound
of st~st~staccato drums
my dr~dr~dribble
hums
right past you.
I b~blast through
and st~st~stutter step
my way through
with crisp
cool
crisscross
crossover moves
I cruise
like a missile
past those
who choose
to snooze
on sk~sk~skills that
abuse
and confuse.

Watch the fire
in my sh-shoes
as I amaze
and b-blaze
a trail
through the m-maze
of obstacles
in my gaze.
When it's time
to excite
I light
and ignite
the torch
and scorch
my foes
with flames
as they choke
on the smoke
that emotes

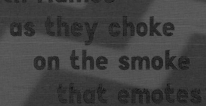

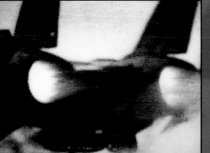

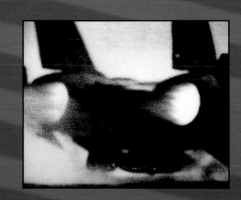

from my **afterburner.**

After I watch a great basketball game, there are moments that just jump out at me when I think about it later. A simple pass to an open man that led to the win-ning point. How one player outjumped everyone else to grab a rebound. The way a player's body jerked every time he dribbled the ball up court. The funny way another player jumped when he shot his jump shot. It's these moments that stick out in my mind when I think about why I enjoyed the game so much. These moments are what I like to call the "short takes" in a game, because they leave an imprint on your mind like a snapshot.

Everyone enjoys watching the game for different reasons. Some like it for the competition. Some like it for the action. Some like it because they enjoy watching guys do things that they can only dream about. *Short Takes* is about those little moments that, for whatever reason, stand out in your mind and are significant.

Finding a way to show these images through photography was a challenge to me. Not only did I want to illustrate what a poem was saying, I also wanted to make the images look dynamic and be "visual jazz" for the words. I wanted to have the images move like a rap song and have different beats, to use them the way a DJ uses records. Many of the images are repeated to make a point. Some are reversed. Some are made bigger. Smaller. Multiplied. Mixed. Basically, anything that would show exactly what the poem is all about. Because poems aren't just words on a page. They are much more than that. Once a poem is created, it is a living, breathing thing; it has life through words. Words that, put together properly, can create worlds that have never been seen, place the reader in the middle of the action, and ultimately take the reader to places he never knew existed.

Now, all of this is not easy. Ideas don't always just pop out of thin air. Inspiration from other things has to play an important part. I drew inspiration from many sources that helped me create the book you now hold in your hands.

For the poetry, I immersed myself in music. I listened to lots of jazz to get a feel for rhythm. From Miles Davis, I learned how to use space and silence. Knowing what to keep in and what to throw out allowed the images to flow. From John Coltrane, I learned how to improvise. The ability to come up with something on the spot and build on it is a great skill that takes lots of practice. I learned how to paint a picture with words by listening to hip-hop artists Jay-Z, A Tribe Called Quest, The Notorious B.I.G., and The Roots. The way they use similes, metaphors, and slang helped me be more creative in the selection of words that I used. By studying a collection of poems titled *Avalanche*, by Quincy Troupe, I learned how a poet combines all these elements and how to use words like musical notes, which gave me a new appreciation of them and their power.

For the images, I looked to movies and music videos. I wanted to have a storytelling element in the pictures but also maintain a creative and expressive side for the images. Movies helped with the storytelling; music videos helped with the visually expressive side. Since the poems contain references to everything from drums to rain to fire, I took images of these things from various sources. Some pictures were taken from videotapes. Some pictures were taken of household objects. Some pictures were taken of things that had to be created specifically for the book. This helped me avoid having to show a million different photos of guys playing basketball and gave the book a unique look. Because in the end, it's not about what you actually see on the court, but what you remember and why you remember it. ⬡

antonym (AN~tuh~nim) a word having a meaning opposite to another word

cadence (KAY~dense) the measure or beat of movement; the pace at which a poem moves

concept (KON~sept) an idea

haiku (HY~koo) a Japanese lyric poem having three unrhymed lines of five, seven, and five syllables; a haiku can be numbered or untitled.

homonym (HOMM~uh~nim) one of two or more words that have the same sound but different meanings (*to, too, two*)

metaphor (MET~a~fore) a figure of speech in which one thing is used to represent another (see "*The Rain~maker*" *and* "*The Predator*")

meter (MEE~ter) the rhythmic pattern of a stanza determined by the kind and number of lines

rhythm (RITH~um) a specific kind of metrical pattern or flow

simile (SIM~a~lee) a comparison of one thing with another, using *like* or *as* ("*I shake and break ankles like sticks.*")

slang words used in place of standard words for effect ("*Cock the hammer and crush the tin.*")

staccato (stuh~CAH~toh) abrupt, discon~nected parts or sounds (see "*After~burner*")

stanza (STANDS~uh) a group of lines in verse

synonym (SIN~uh~nim) a word with nearly the same meaning as another

verse a line of poetry

32